# CORDUROY'S Garden

Story by **Alison Inches**

Illustrations by **Allan Eitzen**

*Based on the characters created by*
**Don Freeman**

**PUFFIN BOOKS**

PUFFIN BOOKS
Published by Penguin Group
Penguin Young Readers Group,
345 Hudson Street, New York, New York 10014, U.S.A.
Penguin Books Ltd, 80 Strand, London WC2R ORL, England
Penguin Books Australia Ltd, 250 Camberwell Road, Camberwell, Victoria 3124, Australia
Penguin Books Canada Ltd, 10 Alcorn Avenue, Toronto, Ontario, Canada M4V 3B2
Penguin Books (N.Z.) Ltd, 182-190 Wairau Road, Auckland 10, New Zealand

First published in the United States of America by Viking,
a division of Penguin Putnam Books for Young Readers, 2002
Published by Puffin Books, a division of Penguin Young Readers Group, 2004

7   9   10   8

Copyright © Penguin Putnam Inc., 2002
Text by Alison Inches
Illustrations by Allan Eitzen
All rights reserved

THE LIBRARY OF CONGRESS HAS CATALOGED THE VIKING EDITION AS FOLLOWS:
Inches, Alison.
Corduroy's garden / written by Alison Inches ; illustrated by Allan Eitzen;
p.   cm.
"Based on the character created by Don Freeman."
Summary: When the beans that Lisa has planted are dug up by a dog, Corduroy
reseeds the garden that he was supposed to be watching, but he and Lisa are
in for a surprise when the "beans" finally appear on the vines.
ISBN: 0-670-03547-5 (hc)
[1. Teddy bears—Fiction. 2. Toys—Fiction. 3. Plants—Fiction. 4. Gardens—Fiction.]
I. Eitzen, Allan, ill.   II. Title.   PZ7.1355   Cn   2002   [E]—dc21   2001007635

Puffin Easy-to-Read ISBN 0-14-240131-5
Puffin® and Easy-to-Read® are registered trademarks of Penguin Group (USA) Inc.

Manufactured in China
Set in Bookman

Reading Level 1.8

# CORDUROY'S Garden

Dig! Dig! Dig!

Plop! Plop! Plop!

Pat! Pat! Pat!

"There!" said Lisa.

"My beans are all planted."

Lisa watered the seeds.

Then she picked up Corduroy.

"Come on, Corduroy," she said.

"I have an important job for you."

She took Corduroy inside

and put him in a chair by the window.

The window had a view of the garden.

"I want you to watch the beans," said Lisa.

Then off she went to school.

"Wow," said Corduroy.

"I get to watch the beans!"

Corduroy got right to work.

He watched and watched.

He saw a man next door raking

and a lady walking her baby.

He saw butterflies and birds

and shapes in the clouds.

Soon, the sun began to feel warm.

Corduroy yawned.

**Ha hum!**

And yawned.

**Ha hum!**

Then Corduroy fell sound asleep.

**Jingle! Jingle! Jingle!**

A puppy pushed open the gate.

Corduroy did not hear the puppy's tags

or the sound of the gate.

The puppy began digging.

**Thwack! Thwack! Thwack!**

Dirt hit the window.

Corduroy woke up

and looked out the window.

His fur stood on end.

"Oh, no!" cried Corduroy.

"The beans!"

**Rap! Rap! Rap!**

Corduroy rapped on the window.

But the puppy kept digging.

**Thwack! Thwack! Thwack!**

And digging.

Then **Plunk!**

The puppy put his bone

in the hole.

**Flick! Flick! Flick!**

He buried it

and left the garden.

Corduroy jumped down from the window.

"I have to find more seeds!" said Corduroy.

Corduroy looked in Lisa's desk.

He looked in a box.

He looked under the bed.

"Why, here are some seeds!" said Corduroy.

Corduroy put three seeds in his pocket
and went to the garden.

**Dig! Dig! Dig!**

**Plop! Plop! Plop!**

**Pat! Pat! Pat!**

"There!" said Corduroy.

"The beans are all replanted."

Corduroy went inside

and climbed back in the window.

"This time," said Corduroy,

"I will watch the beans more carefully."

And he did.

He watched them on sunny days.

He watched them on rainy days.

He watched them on all the days in between.

Soon, three little shoots came up.

They grew and grew.

The stems wrapped around the stakes.

Corduroy kept watching.

The plants grew leaves

and flowers.

Then little beans began to form.

"I see a bean!" said Corduroy.

He clapped his paws.

"I must be getting good at bean watching!"

said Corduroy.

He put on his sunglasses
and got back to work.

Then **Jingle! Jingle! Jingle!**

Corduroy took off his glasses.

*Oh, no!* thought Corduroy.

*The PUPPY!*

The puppy had come back for his bone.

Corduroy blocked the beans.

The puppy stopped and looked at Corduroy.

His ears went up.

"Arf!" said the puppy.

Corduroy shut his eyes.

But the puppy did not take the bone.

He took Corduroy instead!

The puppy played toss with Corduroy.

Corduroy flew up and down,

up and down!

Then the man next door said,

"NO!"

**Thunk!**

Corduroy fell to the ground.

The man picked Corduroy up
and dusted him off.
"I know where you live," said the man.
He took Corduroy home.
And just in time.

**Squeeeeak!**
The school bus stopped out front.

Lisa ran through the garden gate.

"Oh, look!" she cried.

"I see beans on the vine!"

She picked up Corduroy

and ran to see.

Lisa held a bean in her hand.

She turned it from side to side.

Her eyes grew wide.

"Oooh," said Lisa.

"This is *not* a bean!"

*It's not?* thought Corduroy.

*Then what is it?*

"It's a green pepper!" said Lisa.

*A green pepper,* thought Corduroy.

*Is that good?*

"I *love* green peppers!" said Lisa.

*Oh, phew!* thought Corduroy.

"Corduroy, you did a great job."

*I always wanted to do a great job,*

thought Corduroy.